ZAMBI ZEBRA'S STRIPES

Written by **Qi Zhi**

Illustrated by **Cheng Yue**

CARDINAL
MEDIA

Zambi Zebra loves living in the animal kingdom.

He has lots of friends and there is always good food to share.

But sometimes,
Zambi is sad.

Zambi Zebra is the only one in the animal kingdom who has stripes.

Zambi's stripes make him feel *different*. He doesn't like feeling different.

Holly Horse doesn't have stripes.

Hector Hippo doesn't have stripes.

Della Deer has spots, but no stripes.

Nobody else in the animal kingdom
has stripes like Zambi Zebra.

Not Gordy Goat.

Not Greta Goat.

One day, Zambi feels extra sad. He goes for a walk by the pond and there, in the water, he sees an animal with stripes! Just like him! Now he's not different anymore!

"Hello, striped friend!" he says.

But the striped animal doesn't say hello.

The striped animal disappears as soon as Zambi Zebra moves away from the water.

Oh, no! It wasn't a new striped friend after all.
Zambi had only seen his own reflection in the
pond. He feels alone and different again.

Just then, Hannah Hen arrives. "My, my," she says. "I love your stripes! They make you very special, just like the red comb on my head."

Zambi smiles and says, "I never thought about it that way before. My stripes do make me special. Thanks, Hannah Hen!"

Zambi Zebra is so happy about
his special stripes. When he
meets Della Deer, he says,
"I love your spots, Della.
They make you very special."

ISBN 978-1-64074-051-8

Through Jiangsu Phoenix Education Publishing Ltd.

Printed in China

2 4 6 8 10 9 7 5 3 1